CLEVERSTICKS

For Iris and the children of
Cherry Orchard and Thorntree

DRAGONFLY BOOKS PUBLISHED BY CROWN PUBLISHERS, INC.
Text copyright © 1991 by Bernard Ashley
Illustrations copyright © 1991 by Derek Brazell

CROWN is a trademark of Crown Publishers, Inc. Printed in Singapore

Library of Congress Cataloging-in-Publication Data
Ashley, Bernard.
Cleversticks / Bernard Ashley ; illustrated by Derek Brazell.
p. cm.
Summary: Wishing he had something to be clever at like each of the other children
in his class, Ling Sung unexpectedly and happily discovers the others admire his
prowess with chopsticks.
[1. Chopsticks—Fiction. 2. Schools—Fiction. 3. Growth—Fiction.] I. Brazell,
Derek, ill. II. Title.
PZ7.A8262C1   1992
[E]—dc20   91-34669

ISBN 0-517-58878-1 (trade)
0-517-58879-X (lib. bdg.)
0-517-88332-5 (pbk.)

12 13 14 15 16 17 18 19 20

First Dragonfly Books Edition: September 1995

CLEVERSTICKS

by Bernard Ashley

illustrated by
Derek Brazell

Dragonfly Books

CROWN PUBLISHERS, INC. • *New York*

Ling Sung started school on Monday, but on Wednesday morning he decided he didn't want to go anymore.

There were too many things the others could do that he couldn't. Like tying his shoes. Terry could do his, and he kept undoing them and doing them up again while everyone had to watch.

Ling Sung tried to do his, but his fingers got tangled up and the laces kept going their own ways.

Manjit knew how to write her name. She wrote
it on all her things, and she painted it even bigger
than her picture.

Ms. Smith and Ms. Dhanjal clapped, and Manjit
held the painting up for everyone to see.

Ling Sung tried to write his name, too. But he wasn't sure how to do the letters or which way the writing had to go.

The one thing Ling Sung could do came at home time. Very carefully he buttoned up his coat. But when he finished, he had a button left over, and his coat was all up on one side.

Sharon did hers perfectly, and Ms. Smith said wasn't she clever? She didn't say anything about Ling Sung but just did up his coat properly while she talked to Sharon's dad.

Ling Sung didn't want to go to school ever again. He wanted to spend the whole day doing things he liked. Watching the red-nosed clowns in the park. Doing somersaults for the cat.

Splashing his mom at the pool.
And bathing his little sister.

But the next day there he was at school again.
At snack time Anis showed everyone how he
could tie his apron at the back, all by himself.

Ling Sung couldn't even do up the apron with the Velcro tabs. The others said it kept making a rude noise. He turned his back on them. He was fed up with clapping for other people for the things they could do. Why couldn't he be good at something, too?

He saw two long paintbrushes. Someone hadn't put them in their jar.

Ling Sung fiddled with them and didn't pay attention when the cookies came around. He nearly dropped his plate, and his cookie broke into pieces.

Terry pointed at him and laughed.
  "You looked like a clown juggling that
plate," he said.

"Red noses!" said Ling Sung – and made a clown face. He put both the brushes into one hand and chopsticked the cookie pieces into his mouth – the way he ate at home.

Ms. Smith suddenly clapped.

"Oh, look, everyone! Look what Ling Sung
can do! Isn't that clever?"

She was pleased.

"Do it again, Ling Sung," she said.
"Can anyone else use chopsticks?"
No one could.
"Oh, where's the camera?"
said Ms. Dhanjal.

Ling Sung knew just how to hold the
chopsticks, and how to hold his plate
close to his mouth. When he was small, it
had been hard to do, but now he didn't
even think about it.

Everyone wanted to be shown how to do it.
It wasn't easy.

"Show us again, Ling Sung," they shouted.

Ling Sung helped the teachers, too. They were dropping cookie all over the place.

They laughed and tried again.
"I can nearly do it," said Ms. Smith.

Then Ling Sung got them to show him how to do their best things. Manjit helped him with his writing.

"Down and along," she said. "That's an L. And S for Sung is one big snake."

Terry showed Ling Sung how to tie his laces.
" 'Round like this – and don't let go!"

And Sharon told him how to do up his coat. "You don't start in the middle. Start at the top or the bottom, then go down or come up. Easy."

Anis did up Ling Sung's apron for him – so tight he could hardly breathe.

Ling Sung couldn't wait to tell his dad when he met him after school. He could do something that made the others clap!

"A real cleversticks!" his dad said.